To my two little owls, Nayeli and Malachi.
I'm looking forward to a lifetime of
adventure with you two.

Love, Daddy

Choose joy.

Very Bear
and the
Butterfly

Written by David Wise
Illustrated by Harry Lau

Very Bear was a very big and very kind bear.
He lived in a cozy den and had plenty of his favorite
things to eat. Because he had more than enough, Very Bear
was always generous. He shared his food with the hungry and
opened his den to lost animals. He protected the small
creatures when the big ones picked on them.
Very Bear was a very good bear.

One day, Very Bear
caught Slypp the weasel teasing a
pair of mice by dangling blackberries in front
of them only to snatch them up before they could
take a bite. Very Bear lost his temper. It made him sad
when the strong picked on the weak.

"Stop that!" Very Bear said after he exploded from
behind Slypp. "See how it feels to get picked on by
someone bigger than you!" He grabbed her by
the scruff of the neck and hurled her into
the pond.

Slypp hated water, and she was embarrassed. She vowed to get Very Bear back in a very big way.

Slypp knew just what to do! She would ruin Very Bear's hibernation! Everyone knows bears love a full tummy and a nice long sleep.

So she set out to spoil all of Very
Bear's favorite fall food stores. She told the bees to
move their hives to the tall thin aspens so Very Bear
couldn't reach his delicious golden honey.

Slypp followed Very Bear to his secret
berry stash and picked every branch clean of berries.

Every time she saw Very Bear setting
out with his fishing pole, Slypp would scamper to his
fishing spot and scare the fish away.

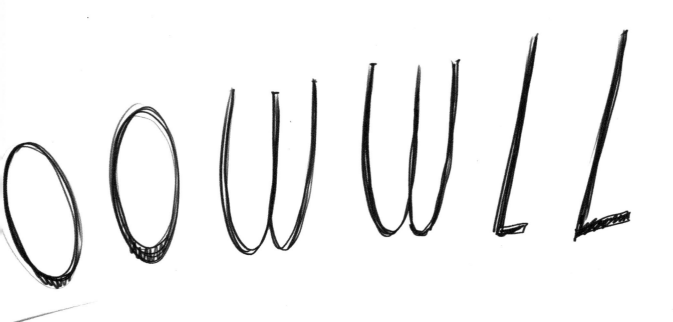

OOWWLL

Rotten apples, half-chewed corn
husks, dry grass, and pine nuts were all Very Bear
could find to fill his tummy before hibernation.
He ended up with enough to eat, but his tummy
didn't feel good about it.

Finally, the time for
hibernation came. Very Bear settled
down in his cozy den. Not long into his slumber,
a family of ground squirrels stumbled in and made a
racket. Slypp had paid them in acorns to be loud and rude,
and they played the part well. No bear likes to be woken
up before spring, especially not over and over again by
chattering squirrels. Very Bear grumbled and swatted
and finally threatened to eat them if they didn't
leave him alone, so the squirrels scattered.

Every week Slypp came up with
a new way to interrupt Very Bear's sleep.

One week she dumped pollen into his den. Very Bear
woke up to the worst sneezing fit he had ever had, and it
was almost a week before he didn't sneeze every time he
rolled over. The next week she lobbed a hornets' nest in
with him. The next week she snuck in and bit his toes
every night. Even worse, Slypp convinced Dave the
skunk to spray the den by offering him her
entire winter supply of pine nuts.

Very Bear had had enough!
He decided that he needed to move, so he
set out in search of a new den. It was a miserably
cold day, and he didn't find the snow fun at all. By the
time he found a new den, he was cold right down to his
bones. But he was so tired he fell right to sleep and
dreamed about **Slypp** laughing her naughty
little head off.

One day Very Bear woke up
sick. He went out for a walk to find some
food and get some fresh air. On the way out of his
cave, he poked his eye with a clump of pine needles and
stubbed his right paw while stumbling around trying to
recover from his pine blindness.

It made Very Bear very angry indeed!

He stormed through the
forest, breaking logs, smashing nests,
and hurling pinecones at any creature silly
enough to come in range of his paws. He was mad,
and he was going to make sure that the whole
forest knew it.

Then something extraordinary
happened. The most beautiful butterfly the forest
had ever seen came floating along. Her name was Flutters,
and you could tell just by looking at her that she was
a kind butterfly.

Very Bear's fury caught her eye, and
she stopped to watch him. But the bear was too busy
feeling sorry for himself to notice the butterfly. Flutters noticed
Very Bear's frustration and decided to help. It feels great to cheer
anyone up, but it feels even better to cheer up a very big,
very grumpy bear.

As Flutters drifted down
to land on Very Bear's nose, he stood
still and watched her. Grumpily, he shook
his head furiously to knock her off. Flutters
held on tight. Surprised, Very Bear smiled
and shook harder. This butterfly was
challenging his bearliness!

He shook and nodded his
head harder, and still she held on. He
shook, jumped, and danced even harder, but
the butterfly stayed stuck to his nose like glue. Very
Bear's nose started to tickle. He started to tumble around
and bump into things. Soon the whole forest was busy
watching the dance of the butterfly and the bear.

Eventually Very Bear collapsed on the forest floor in
a fit of laughter. Flutters was laughing too, and
together they laughed and laughed.

Flutters showed him her favorite spots and opened his eyes to a beauty that he hadn't noticed because he was too busy looking down at the ground in search of food. He had been so busy worrying about himself that he missed all the beauty that was happening around him.

"Very Bear, why were
you so mad when I first found
you this morning?" Flutters asked.

Very Bear explained all about the weasel
and his rough winter.

"It sounds to me like you let the weasel win."
Flutters sighed.

"Humph! That's not true!"
growled Very Bear.

"Yes it is," explained
Flutters. "Grumpy, angry,
and frustrated is exactly how Slypp
wanted you to feel. She made you so mad you
forgot who you are. Where is the kind, generous,
protective bear I know is inside?"

"But so many bad things happened to me, and I was
so hungry." Very Bear sighed.

"You are right that many bad things happened to you,
and you can't control that. But you can control how you
react to the things that happen to you. How long did it take
you to realize Slypp was messing with you?"

"I knew right from the start that she was behind it all."

"So you could have asked her for forgiveness?"

"Forgiveness! Bah! She got what she
deserved! She was being mean to
the mice," Very Bear stated.

"Did you ask how the mice felt
about it? Maybe they were actually enjoying it;
maybe they thought it was a game. Slypp didn't always
pull the berries away in time."

Very Bear sat quietly and pondered what Flutters
had said. Maybe he was just as wrong as
the weasel had been.

"Remember, Very Bear, even if
others are mean to you, only you can decide how
you are going to feel about it. You are a big, tough, and
kind bear. I think you can stand up to the pranks of a
sneaky weasel without losing your temper."

Very Bear was
humbled. He knew in his heart that she
was right, and he promised to be his kind, joyful
self no matter what happened to him.

Very Bear tried hard to be kinder to his forest friends. He
shared his food and let any needy creature share his den. His
friends loved Very Bear more than ever, and they made sure
he had enough to eat. Slypp even learned to respect
Very Bear, and they became friends.

The butterfly and the bear
were the best of friends and hardly ever apart.
They went on many adventures together, and Very Bear
was always thankful for the day when a winged beauty
decided to land on his nose.

children LEADING children™

WITH SPECIAL THANKS TO THE ENTIRE CHILDREN LEADING CHILDREN COMMUNITY

CREDITS:

Written by: David Wise

Illustration by: Harry Lau

Designed by: AuthorPackages.com

Editing Services by: Rebecca Maxfield

Creative Direction by: LaRae Wright

Library of Congress Control Number: 2017958706

ISBN: 978-0-9994474-3-7